To Dan,
Tom, & Sarah—
for their footprints in the snow

Henry Holt and Company, LLC
Publishers since 1866
175 Fifth Avenue
New York, New York 10010
www.HenryHoltKids.com

Henry Holt® is a registered trademark of Henry Holt and Company, LLC.
Copyright © 2007 by Mei Matsuoka
First published in the United States in 2008 by Henry Holt and Company, LLC
Originally published in Great Britain in 2007 by Andersen Press Ltd.
All rights reserved. Distributed in Canada by H. B. Fenn and Company Ltd.

Library of Congress Control Number: 2007938929

ISBN-13: 978-0-8050-8792-5 / ISBN-10: 0-8050-8792-3

First American Edition—2008
Printed in Singapore.
1 3 5 7 9 10 8 6 4 2

Footprints in the Snow

mei matsuoka

Henry Holt and Company • New York

It was a cold winter's day.

Wolf sat by the fire in his cozy little house,

reading all the books he had about wolves.

All the wolves in the stories that he read

were **nasty,**

SCARY,

and **greedy.**

"I think it's time somebody wrote a story about a NICE wolf," he said.

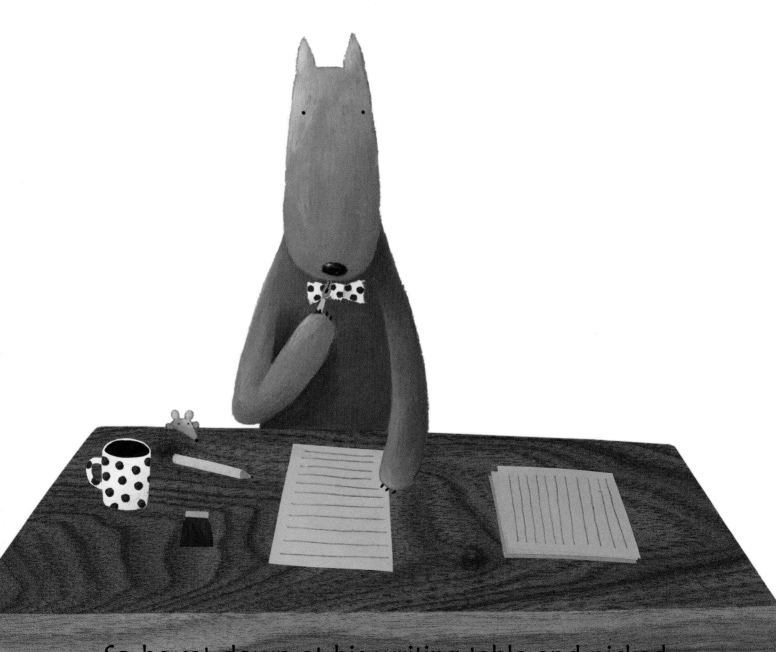

So he sat down at his writing table and picked up a pen. And this is how the story went . . .

One winter's morning,

it snowed and

snowed and snowed and snowed.

When it finally stopped snowing, Mr. Nice Wolf stepped out of his house to go for a walk.

In the silk-smooth bed of snow, he spotted some footprints leading into the forest. "Hmmm, I wonder whose those could be?" he thought.

He decided to follow
the footprints to find out
who they belonged to so that
he could make a new friend.

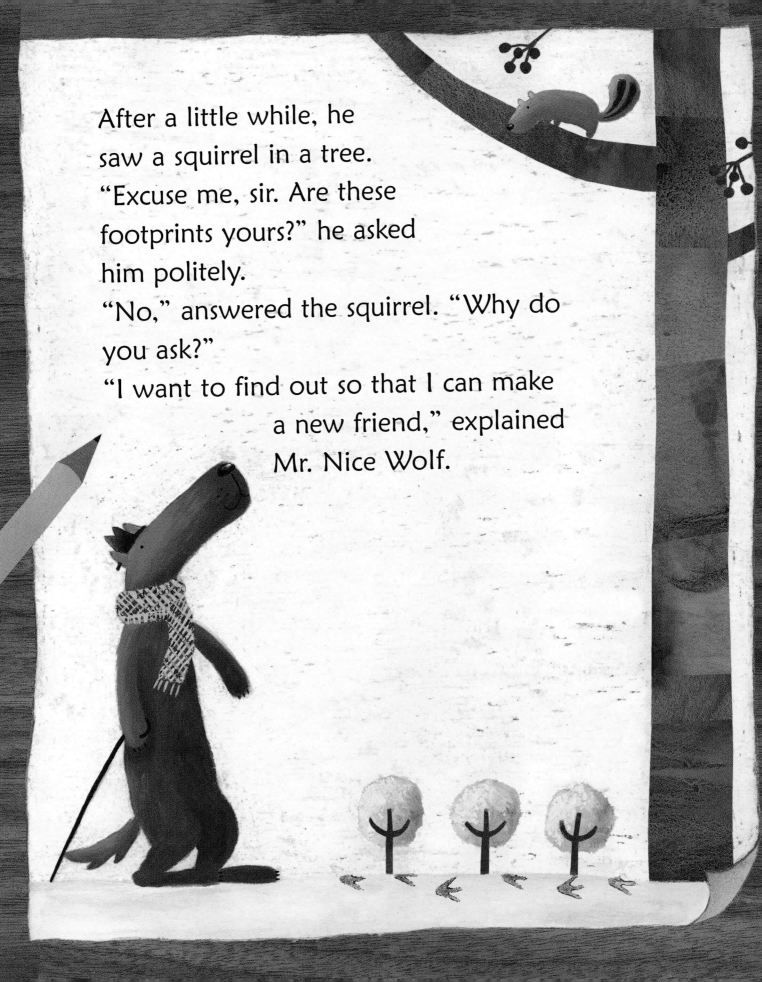

After a little while, he
saw a squirrel in a tree.
"Excuse me, sir. Are these
footprints yours?" he asked
him politely.
"No," answered the squirrel. "Why do
you ask?"
"I want to find out so that I can make
a new friend," explained
Mr. Nice Wolf.

"I don't believe you,"

said the squirrel.

"You just want to find out

so that you can EAT the poor thing!"

And with that he scampered off.

Next, Mr. Nice Wolf came across
a bunny rabbit poking her nose out
of her burrow. "Excuse me, madam.
Are these footprints yours?"
he asked her cheerfully.
"I want to find out so that
I can make a new friend."

"I don't believe you," said the rabbit.
"You're just hungry and you want
to find some BREAKFAST!"
And with that she hopped
back down into her burrow.

Mr. Nice Wolf (who wasn't feeling too nice at all by this point) tried to ignore what she said and carried on. He soon came to a big lake in the middle of the forest.

CROAK, CROAK!

"Oh, could these footprints be yours?"
Mr. Wolf asked the frog.

"No," said the frog. "And there's no way I would tell you whose they are, even if I knew!"

Then he dived into the lake and swam off.

Right over on the other side of the lake,
Mr. Wolf saw a big brown duck.

"Hello there!"

he shouted.

"These must be YOUR footprints!" he said.
"Yes," answered the duck, swimming over.
"Oh good! I've been looking for you," said
Mr. Wolf. "I was hoping we could be—"

But as he spoke Mr. Wolf took a good long look
at the duck and forgot all about
what he was saying.

For the duck looked
so fat, juicy, . . .

and mouthwateringly TASTY. . .

Wolf was startled to find himself
back in his own house!

"Pheeew!

I almost let my story end with Mr. Nice Wolf being just as bad as all the other wolves!"

Wolf got out of the bath to dry himself off when suddenly there was a knock at the door.

KNOCK KNOCK! KNOCK KNOCK!

"I'M COMING, I'M COMING!"

Wolf called.

He opened the door...

... and in the silk-smooth bed of snow, he spotted

some footprints! "Hmmm. I wonder whose those could be?"